WHEN GODS WALKED THE SACRED HILLS

LEGENDS OF SESHACHALAM

YS YADAV

To the enduring memory of my beloved father,

YAMANABOINA MUNIRAJ YADAV (Late),

You were the architect of my spirit, a guiding star in the vast
expanse of my life. More than a father, you were my mentor, my
compass, and the unwavering beacon that illuminated my path.
Though your physical presence departed in my formative years,
your wisdom continues to resonate, a timeless melody that shapes
my journey.

Your narratives, imbued with profound insight, were not mere tales; they were profound windows into the essence of existence. You taught me the art of attentive listening, the courage to question, the wisdom to understand, and the purpose to live with intention. Through your stories, you unveiled the extraordinary within the ordinary, instilling in me the ability to seek meaning in every moment and to honor the rich tapestry of heritage that defines us.

This narrative, one of the countless treasures you bestowed upon me, reflects the depth of your understanding, the power of your imagination, and the profound truths you conveyed. Your tales were not mere recollections; they were lessons of love, resilience, unwavering faith, and a life lived with purpose.

This book stands as a humble tribute to you, not only to the exceptional father you were but also to the enduring legacy of inspiration and love you have bequeathed to the world.

With everlasting gratitude and deepest reverence,

Your son,

Y.S. Yadav

Contents

Acknowledgements

A Confluence of Blessings

This book, a heartfelt endeavor born from the seeds of cherished memories and unwavering devotion, would not have blossomed without the confluence of countless blessings, both seen and unseen. It is a tapestry woven from threads of inspiration, unwavering support, and the gentle guidance of those who have illuminated my path.

First and foremost, I extend my deepest and most profound gratitude to my beloved father, late. Y. Muniraj Yadav. His voice, a beacon of wisdom and warmth, echoed through the ancient banyan, weaving tales that ignited my imagination and instilled within me a profound reverence for the sacred legacy of Tirupati. His stories, far exceeding the boundaries of mere narratives, were profound lessons in devotion, resilience, and the eternal bond between humanity and the divine. This book stands as a humble testament to his enduring spirit and the timeless wisdom he so generously imparted.

To the divine grace that permeates the sacred hills of Seshachalam, I offer my heartfelt obeisance. The temples of Tirumala and Tirupati, living embodiments of faith and devotion, have served as a constant source of inspiration and spiritual sustenance throughout this journey. Their enduring presence, a testament to the power of unwavering belief, has guided me through the intricacies of this narrative.

I am profoundly grateful to the countless scholars, historians, and devotees whose meticulous research and unwavering dedication have preserved the rich history and cultural heritage of these hallowed sites. Their painstaking work has provided the essential foundation upon which this narrative is built, ensuring that the stories of Tirupati are shared with authenticity and profound respect.

To my family, whose unwavering support and boundless encouragement have been a constant source of strength, I express my deepest and most sincere appreciation. Their understanding and patience have allowed me to dedicate the necessary time and energy to this labor of love.

To the editors and publishers who have brought this book to fruition, I extend my heartfelt thanks. Their expertise, dedication, and keen eye have transformed my words into a cohesive and compelling narrative, ensuring that the stories of Tirupati reach a wider audience.

To the priests and temple authorities of Tirumala and Tirupati, whose dedication preserves the daily rituals and traditions, thank you for your service.

And finally, to you, the reader, I offer my sincere gratitude. Your interest and engagement in these sacred stories are the ultimate reward for this endeavor. May this book inspire you to explore the rich tapestry of our cultural heritage, to embrace the enduring power of faith, and to cherish the timeless wisdom that binds us all together in the grand tapestry of existence.

This book is not merely a product of my individual effort; it is a collective offering, a testament to the enduring power of community, faith, and the enduring legacy of stories that transcend time and space. May it serve as a gentle reminder that the divine is present in every aspect of our lives, and that the stories we share have the power to illuminate our path and guide us towards a more enlightened future.

Preface

Echoes of the Timeless Banyan

Countless narratives have woven themselves around the origins and enduring legacy of the temples of Tirupati and Tirumala. Each, in its own unique way, carries a spark of beauty, a depth of insight, and a profound connection to the divine. Yet, this book is not merely another scholarly chronicle of these revered sanctuaries. It is, at its heart, a deeply personal odyssey—a tapestry woven from the stories entrusted to me by my father nearly four decades ago, beneath the sheltering canopy of an ancient banyan tree.

These were not simply tales spun from the threads of mythology and history; they were profound lessons in unwavering devotion, indomitable resilience, and the eternal, unbreakable bond between humanity and the divine. My father, Late. Y. Muniraj Yadav, through the art of his storytelling, masterfully connected the intricate threads of our shared history, our rich spirituality, and our vibrant cultural essence, breathing life into them in a way that resonated deeply within my soul. His narratives wove together the sacred moments of Lord Krishna, Balarama, and Sukamuni, and illuminated the visionary dedication of those who preserved these hallowed sites for generations to come.

This book, born from the cherished memories of those twilight evenings spent with my father, ventures beyond the mere architectural grandeur of Tirupati's temples. It delves into the profound purpose they serve—then, now, and for all time. It explores their historical significance, their spiritual essence, and the timeless lessons they offer to humanity, lessons that transcend the boundaries of time and culture. It is a humble endeavor to preserve and share the enduring legacy of these sacred temples and the stories my father so lovingly passed down to me, ensuring that they continue to illuminate the path for generations to come.

As you embark on this literary pilgrimage through these pages, you will witness how the temples of Tirupati are far more than mere architectural marvels. They are living, breathing symbols of divine grace, unwavering strength, and the boundless cosmic energy that permeates the universe. They are vibrant centers of devotion, cultural preservation, and selfless service, bridging the chasm between past and present, connecting the mortal realm to the eternal divine.

This book is dedicated to my father, whose words continue to guide me like a celestial beacon, and to all the parents who, through the timeless art of storytelling, instill enduring values and nurture the souls of their children. May these pages serve as a gentle reminder of the paramount importance of preserving our rich heritage, honoring the wisdom of our ancestors, and embracing the divine presence that graces our daily lives. May they ignite within you a spark of understanding, a flame of devotion, and a deep appreciation for the sacred legacy that binds us all together.

Introduction

Whispers of Seshachalam - A Timeless Pilgrimage

The Temples of Tirumala and Tirupati, etched against the azure canvas of the Andhra sky, are not mere architectural marvels, silent sentinels of a bygone era. They are vibrant, living embodiments of a profound spiritual odyssey, a journey that transcends the ephemeral boundaries of time and space. Their towering gopurams, piercing the heavens like celestial beacons, and their serene sanctums, imbued with an ethereal tranquility, whisper tales of unwavering devotion, indomitable resilience, and divine intervention. They stand as a testament to humanity's eternal, yearning quest for the divine, a testament to the enduring legacy of those who, with unwavering faith and visionary dedication, shaped their sacred history.

This book is an invitation to embark on a pilgrimage to the very heart of these hallowed temples. It is a quest to trace their ancient origins, to unravel their profound significance, and to glean the timeless lessons they offer to a world in constant flux. It is a narrative tapestry woven from the threads of mythology, history, and unwavering devotion, bringing to vivid life the sacred landscapes of Seshachalam, where the divine footsteps of Lord Krishna, Balarama, and Sukamuni once graced the earth.

The chapters that follow are more than mere historical accounts, dry recitations of dates and events. They are reflections of divine grace, unwavering strength, and the boundless cosmic energy that permeates the universe. Each temple, from the serene Alaga Perumal Kovil to the majestic Tirumala Temple, carries its own unique and captivating story, intricately interwoven with the lives of the Yadava kings, the visionary saints like Ramanujacharya, and the countless devotees who have found solace and spiritual sustenance within their sacred precincts.

As you turn these pages, you will journey through the vibrant tapestry of sacred rituals, the grand spectacle of celestial festivals, and the profound cultural impact of these timeless temples. You will witness their remarkable evolution, from humble centers of devotion to formidable pillars of contemporary society, offering vital education, selfless social service, and a unifying force in a world often fragmented by division.

This book is not merely about the temples themselves; it is about the enduring values they embody, the timeless principles they uphold. It is about the transformative power of storytelling, the paramount importance of preserving our rich heritage, and the sacred role of parents in passing down these invaluable lessons to their children. It is a poignant reminder that the divine is not confined to the hallowed halls of temples but resides within the very fabric of the connections we forge, the stories we share, and the lives we lead.

Through these pages, I extend an invitation to perceive the temples of Tirupati not merely as sacred sites, but as profound reflections of humanity's highest ideals, as mirrors reflecting the divine spark that resides within each and every one of us. Let this journey inspire you to honor the divine within and around you, to cherish the sacred connections that bind us together, and to preserve the enduring legacy of faith, culture, and unwavering devotion for generations yet to come.

Prologue

A Father's Tale - Beneath the Timeless Banyan

The air beneath the ancient banyan pulsed with a profound, almost tangible serenity. Its gnarled branches, reaching outwards and upwards, seemed to embody the very essence of time itself, a living testament to the enduring flow of history. This hallowed space, nestled amidst the foothills of Seshachalam, was our sanctuary, a sacred haven where my father, a man of quiet wisdom and boundless warmth, shared narratives that resonated with the weight and wonder of ages past.

As the sun, a molten orb of gold, dipped below the undulating silhouette of the Seshachalam hills, casting long, ethereal shadows across the earth, my young mind, brimming with curiosity, yearned for the unfolding of another captivating tale.

"Shanmukha," my father began, his voice as steady and reassuring as the gentle rustling of the banyan's leaves, "what I am about to share with you is more than a mere story. It is a legacy, a profound truth veiled by the mists of time, waiting to be rediscovered." He paused, his gaze meeting mine, his eyes reflecting the depth of his conviction. "This is the saga of gods and sages, of kings and unwavering devotion—a tale woven into the very fabric of the sacred hills we call home."

Little did I know that this particular evening, bathed in the golden hues of twilight, would forever alter my perception of the world. My father's words, imbued with a captivating eloquence, painted vivid tapestries of Balarama's sacred pilgrimage, Sukamuni's divine vision, and the celestial significance of the temples that graced the Tirupati landscape. Each narrative, shared beneath the sheltering embrace of that ancient banyan, served as a portal into a realm where mythology and history intertwined seamlessly, where the divine walked among mortals, leaving indelible footprints upon the earth.

This book, a labor of love and a testament to cherished memories, is a tribute to those magical evenings, to the stories that my father so lovingly and meticulously passed down, and to the hallowed hills of Seshachalam, which have stood as silent witnesses to centuries of unwavering devotion and divine grace. It is not merely a recounting of historical events; it is a profound journey into the very heart of a living legacy, a legacy that continues to inspire and uplift the souls of countless pilgrims.

May these stories, shared between a father and his son beneath the timeless embrace of an ancient banyan, resonate within your heart as they did within mine, igniting a spark of understanding, wonder, and unwavering faith. May they serve as a gentle reminder of the enduring power of heritage, the profound beauty of devotion, and the timeless wisdom that binds us all together in the grand tapestry of existence.

CHAPTER ONE

BALARAMA'S PILGRIMAGE

The air, thick with the scent of sandalwood and temple flowers, hung still beneath the ancient banyan, a silent witness to our conversation. From its sprawling branches, dappled sunlight filtered down, illuminating the dust motes dancing in the golden rays. My father's voice, a calm, resonant tone, broke the stillness, weaving a tapestry of ancient wisdom. "Shanmukha," he began, his gaze holding mine with an intensity that seemed to transcend time, "Balarama, Krishna's elder brother, was a man defined not only by his formidable strength, but by an unwavering adherence to the principles of dharma. During the tumultuous Kurukshetra War, while Krishna guided Arjuna's strategic path, Balarama chose a different, solitary path—a pilgrimage, a journey of inner exploration and profound introspection."

I tilted my head, the questions of youth bubbling within me. "But Father, why did he turn away from the battlefield? Was it not his duty to stand with his family?"

A gentle, knowing smile touched my father's lips, his eyes reflecting the deep wisdom of generations. "Ah, Shanmukha, duty is a complex and nuanced concept, often extending beyond the immediacy of conflict. Balarama perceived the Kurukshetra War as a tragic manifestation of human folly, a failure to uphold the sacred principles of dharma. He chose to seek understanding and peace rather than participate in the ensuing carnage, embarking on a pilgrimage of reflection."

The Pilgrimage Commences from Dwaraka

"Where did his journey begin, Father?" I asked, my curiosity piqued by the unfolding narrative.

"His pilgrimage commenced from Dwaraka," my father recounted, his voice imbued with the gravitas of an ancient storyteller. "The capital of the Yadava dynasty, his shared kingdom with Krishna. With a profound sense of sorrow, he bid farewell to his people, embarking on a solitary quest for spiritual enlightenment."

"Why did he choose Dwaraka as his starting point, Father?" I pressed, seeking deeper insight.

"Dwaraka was his anchor, his point of existential grounding," he explained, his voice resonating with a sense of profound understanding. "Leaving it symbolized his detachment from worldly ties, his unwavering commitment to the pursuit of eternal dharma, a path we, here in the shadow of the Tirumala hills, still revere."

Sacred Waypoints Along the Pilgrim's Path

"From Dwaraka," my father continued, his voice painting vivid images of the ancient landscape, "Balarama journeyed to the sacred banks of the Yamuna River. The river's holy waters evoked poignant memories of his youth with Krishna. He offered prayers, seeking solace and strength for his arduous journey."

"And what transpired next, Father?" I urged, eager to follow the unfolding narrative.

"He reached Prayag, the confluence of the Ganga, Yamuna, and Saraswati rivers," my father narrated, his tone imbued with reverence. "This hallowed site, where three sacred rivers converge, holds immense spiritual significance. Balarama meditated there, contemplating the delicate balance of dharma amidst the chaos he had left behind, a meditation echoed in the quiet contemplation of the sages who still walk these hills."

Through Verdant Sanctuaries and to the Shores of Rameswaram

"From Prayag, Balarama ventured into the verdant sanctuaries of Bharatavarsha," my father recounted, his voice painting a picture of ancient forests. "He sought the wisdom of meditating sages within secluded ashrams, places where the air itself seemed to vibrate with divine energy."

"Did he encounter anyone of significance, Father?" I asked, picturing the solitary traveler amidst the ancient trees.

A gentle smile played on my father's lips. "Not in the conventional sense, Shanmukha. The forests themselves were his companions, offering solitude and a profound connection with the divine, much like the solitude one can find in the forests surrounding Tirumala."

"Eventually, Balarama reached Rameswaram, where he offered prayers to Lord Shiva. He sought to comprehend the cosmic equilibrium—creation, preservation, and destruction—by the vast expanse of the sea."

"Why Shiva, Father?" I inquired, intrigued by the choice of deity.

"Shiva embodies the eternal cycle of transformation," he explained, his voice imbued with philosophical depth. "By invoking Shiva's blessings, Balarama acknowledged the interconnectedness of all existence. It was a moment of profound humility, a recognition that even the mightiest must submit to the divine order, a lesson as timeless as the stones of the Tirumala hills."

The Arrival at Sukamuni Ashram

"Following his sojourn in Rameswaram, Balarama continued his odyssey through what we now know as Andhra Pradesh," my father narrated, his voice painting a landscape of tranquility. "A land of dense forests and serene rivers, home to sages living in communion with nature. He eventually reached the foothills of the Seshachalam hills, these very hills we stand upon, now known as the Tirumala hills, and discovered Sukamuni Ashram."

"What was the nature of this sanctuary, Father?" I asked, visualizing the secluded retreat.

"It was a haven of tranquility," he replied, his voice filled with reverence. "Towering trees formed a natural canopy, the air alive with the symphony of nature. The ashram, nestled at the foothills of Seshachalam, resonated with divine energy. Sukamuni, a sage of profound wisdom, welcomed Balarama as a cherished guest, understanding the weight he carried."

The Genesis of a Spiritual Legacy

"What did Balarama undertake at the ashram, Father?" I asked softly, sensing the significance of the place.

"He engaged in deep meditation, Shanmukha," my father said simply. "He sought answers to the profound questions that burdened his soul. Sukamuni provided guidance, imparting insights into the eternal principles of dharma and the cosmic balance, insights that have shaped the very spiritual fabric of this region."

He paused, his tone becoming reflective. "But Sukamuni was equally inspired by Balarama's presence, recognizing a strength tempered by humility. And it was within the serene confines of this ashram, here in these very hills, that Balarama began to lay the foundation for a spiritual legacy."

The Thread of Continuity

"And what unfolded next, Father?" I asked, my anticipation heightened.

"That, my dear Shanmukha," he replied, a knowing twinkle in his eye, "is the enduring narrative of Sukamuni Ashram itself—a place that would profoundly influence the sacred temples we hold in reverence today, a story that continues to resonate within the very stones of Tirupati."

CHAPTER TWO

THE TRANQUILITY OF SUKAMUNI ASHRAM

The ancient banyan, a silent guardian of our shared history, swayed gently, its leaves rustling in a soft cadence that seemed to echo my father's words. His voice, imbued with the wisdom of ages, resonated with a profound truth. "Shanmukha," he continued, his gaze holding mine with unwavering intensity, "when Balarama arrived at Sukamuni Ashram, he was guided not merely by astute counsel, but by the very hand of destiny. It was within this tranquil sanctuary that his pilgrimage assumed a divine purpose, shaping the sacred narrative of Seshachalam."

"What kind of place was Sukamuni Ashram, Father?" I asked, leaning forward, my youthful curiosity piqued.

A Sanctuary of Divine Resonance

"Sukamuni Ashram," my father began, his voice painting a vivid portrait of the serene landscape, "was nestled at the foothills of the Seshachalam hills, a sanctuary enveloped by a forest so dense and vibrant that it seemed to hum with divine energy. The ancient trees, towering like silent sentinels, stood as guardians of the sacred space, while a crystalline brook meandered nearby, its gentle murmur a continuous hymn of devotion. The air was thick with the intoxicating fragrance of sandalwood and wild jasmine, a sensory tapestry of tranquility."

He paused, his voice softening, a hint of reverence in his tone. "But what truly distinguished the ashram was the presence of Sukamuni himself."

The Sage of Profound Mystical Wisdom

"Who was Sukamuni, Father?" I asked, captivated by the unfolding tale.

"Sukamuni," my father explained, his voice imbued with a sense of wonder, "was no ordinary sage. He was the son of Vyasa, the venerable compiler of the Vedas and author of the Mahabharata. His story began even before his birth, a tale woven with threads of divine intervention. In his previous incarnation, Sukamuni was a parrot who inadvertently overheard Lord Shiva revealing the secret of immortality to Parvati. Fearing Shiva's divine wrath, the parrot sought refuge in the womb of Vyasa's wife, where he remained for twelve years."

A faint smile graced my father's lips, his tone reverent. "When Sukamuni finally emerged into the world, he did so as an enlightened being, possessing the profound wisdom of the cosmos. His very presence radiated tranquility, and his words carried the essence of divine truth."

"And he welcomed Balarama, Father?" I asked, eager to confirm the connection.

"Indeed," he replied, his voice affirming the divine confluence. "Sukamuni welcomed Balarama with open arms, recognizing the divine aura that enveloped him. Their meeting was not a mere coincidence, but a convergence of destinies, a pivotal moment in the sacred history of these hills."

Sculptures of Celestial Origin

"But what did Balarama do within the ashram, Father?" I asked, my curiosity growing.

"He immersed himself in deep meditation, Shanmukha," my father explained, "reflecting under Sukamuni's guidance, seeking clarity and understanding. However, his divine purpose extended beyond the ashram's boundaries. Guided by his profound devotion, Balarama ventured into the sacred landscapes of Seshachalam."

"Where did he journey?" I asked, my curiosity piqued.

"There, he crafted the first of his divine sculptures—a stone vigraham of Krishna as Partha Sarathi, capturing the essence of his role as the divine charioteer and guide during the Kurukshetra War. And then, at the summit of the Seshachalam hills, Balarama sculpted Krishna in his Viswaroopa, the cosmic form that symbolizes infinity and the boundless expanse of the universe."

The Enigma of the Shaligram Stones

"But Father," I asked, tilting my head in confusion, "where did he procure the stone for these sculptures? The forest doesn't yield such stone, does it?"

My father's eyes gleamed with a sense of wonder. "Ah, Shanmukha, therein lies the profound mystery. Balarama utilized Shaligram stones to create these idols, a material not of earthly origin. It is said that Shaligram stones are fragments of the divine, formed in the sacred waters of the celestial realms."

"Then how did he obtain them?" I asked, my voice a mixture of awe and disbelief.

"No one can definitively say," my father replied, his tone hushed with reverence. "Some posit that he summoned them through his divine power, invoking the energies of the cosmos to bring these sacred stones to Earth. Others believe they were celestial gifts, bestowed upon him as he sculpted. What we do know, Shanmukha, is that these stones radiated a divine energy unlike anything the world had ever witnessed."

Sanctification by Sukamuni's Vision

"Did Balarama return the sculptures to the ashram?" I asked.

"No," my father said softly, his voice resonating with a sense of divine purpose. "Upon completing the sculptures, Balarama left them in the very locations where they were created—at the foothills and the summit of Seshachalam. It was Sukamuni who later visited these sites. Moved by their profound divine energy, he sanctified them as places of worship."

He paused, his voice filled with awe. "Sukamuni perceived the Partha Sarathi vigraham as a symbol of divine guidance and the Viswaroopa as a representation of infinity. He declared that these sites would remain eternally sacred, drawing devotees seeking the divine."

A Land of Eternal Devotion

"And what became of Sukamuni's ashram, Father?" I asked.

"It remained a sanctuary of tranquility," he said. "But the sites he sanctified, the plains and the summit, evolved into pilgrimage destinations, attracting devotees from far and wide. Over time, these sites blossomed into centers of devotion, laying the foundation for the temples we now revere here in Tirupati."

He leaned back, his expression thoughtful. "The confluence of Balarama's profound devotion and Sukamuni's divine blessings transformed Seshachalam into a land of eternal worship, a place where the divine continues to resonate."

A Story for the Twilight Hours

My young mind swirled with images of Shaligram stones, sacred sculptures, and Sukamuni's profound blessings. "What became of the sculptures, Father?" I asked, unable to contain my curiosity.

"That, my dear Shanmukha," he said with a gentle smile, "is a tale for the twilight hours, a story to be savored another evening. But remember this, the energy of those sculptures, born of divine stone and sacred intent, continues to resonate within the very stones of Tirupati's temples, a living testament to the divine."

As the evening shadows lengthened, the stars above seemed to bless the unfolding narrative. My heart was filled with awe and anticipation for the stories yet to be told, the divine mysteries yet to be unveiled.

CHAPTER THREE

Sculpting the Universal Form

The banyan's leaves, bathed in the soft, filtered light of the setting sun, cast an intricate tapestry of shadows, as my father leaned forward, his voice a hushed reverence. "Shanmukha," he began, his gaze holding mine with a profound intensity, "the two sculptures Balarama created were not mere artistic expressions. They were acts of profound devotion, imbued with the very essence of the cosmos, eternal symbols of Krishna's divine manifestation."

I tilted my head, my youthful curiosity evident. "How did he sculpt them, Father? And what made them so extraordinary?"

The Plains of Seshachalam: Partha Sarathi, the Divine Guide

My father's gaze drifted into the distance, as if he were replaying an ancient tableau. "Balarama commenced his divine work on the plains of the Seshachalam forest. The vast, open expanse of the land evoked the battlefield of Kurukshetra—a place where Krishna's guidance as Partha Sarathi illuminated Arjuna's path, a beacon of dharma amidst the chaos."

"Why did he choose that particular spot, Father?" I inquired.

"Because," my father replied, his voice resonating with a deep understanding, "Balarama recognized that Krishna's role as Partha Sarathi was not confined to Arjuna alone. It was a universal message, a reminder that the divine is ever-present, guiding humanity through life's trials and tribulations."

He paused, his voice filled with awe. "Using the celestial Shaligram stone, Balarama sculpted Krishna in the form of the divine charioteer. Each stroke of his chisel was a prayer, each intricate detail an offering. The vigraham captured Krishna's serene countenance, his unwavering strength, and the profound wisdom disseminated through the Bhagavad Gita, a timeless testament to divine guidance."

The Summit of Seshachalam: Viswaroopa, the Cosmic Manifestation

"And then he ascended to the summit of Seshachalam," my father continued, his voice rising in reverence. "Standing at the highest point, closer to the heavens, Balarama felt the boundless energy of the cosmos. It was there that he embarked on his second creation—the Viswaroopa."

"What is the Viswaroopa, Father?" I asked, my voice a blend of curiosity and wonder.

"It is Krishna's cosmic form," he explained, his eyes gleaming with an inner light. "The Viswaroopa represents the infinite energy of the universe, the eternal cycle of creation, preservation, and dissolution that exists in perfect equilibrium. It is the awe-inspiring form that Krishna revealed to Arjuna, unveiling the vastness and majesty of the divine."

My father's eyes shimmered as he painted a vivid picture of the scene. "With his hands guided by unwavering devotion, Balarama sculpted Krishna as the Viswaroopa. The Shaligram stone seemed to radiate an ethereal light as the cosmic form took shape—immense in its power, yet serene in its harmonious balance."

The Enigmatic Origins of the Celestial Stones

"Father," I asked, "how did Balarama obtain the Shaligram stone for these extraordinary sculptures?"

My father smiled, his expression imbued with thoughtful contemplation. "That, Shanmukha, remains a question shrouded in mystery. The Shaligram stone is not found on Earth—it is a celestial material, infused with divine energy. Some surmise that Balarama summoned it from the depths of the cosmos, utilizing his divine powers. Others believe it was a celestial gift, bestowed upon him in recognition of his profound devotion."

He leaned closer, his voice a soft murmur. "What we do know, Shanmukha, is that these stones carried the very essence of the cosmos. They were not mere stone, but conduits of divine energy, alive with the spirit of the universe."

Sukamuni's Pilgrimage to the Divine Sculptures

"Upon completing the vigrahams," my father continued, "Balarama left them in their respective locations—one on the plains, the other at the summit. He did not return them to Sukamuni Ashram.

Instead, it was Sukamuni who later journeyed to these sacred sites."

"Why did he undertake this pilgrimage, Father?" I asked.

"Sukamuni," my father replied, "was guided by a divine vision, an inner call to witness the fruits of Balarama's devotion. Upon beholding the sculptures, he was overcome with profound reverence. He recognized them as tangible manifestations of Krishna's divinity, crafted with boundless love and devotion. And so, he sanctified these hallowed sites, declaring them eternally sacred."

Eternal Symbols of Divine Presence

"Sukamuni's blessings transformed these locations," my father said. "The plains, where the Partha Sarathi vigraham stood, became a shrine of divine guidance, a constant reminder of Krishna's role as the charioteer of dharma. The summit, where the Viswaroopa radiated its cosmic energy, became a beacon of infinity, a place where the divine and the universe converged as one."

"And what became of the sculptures, Father?" I asked.

"They remained there for generations," he replied. "Pilgrims who visited these sacred sites carried their stories across vast lands, spreading the sanctity of Seshachalam. Over time, these locations evolved into centers of profound devotion, laying the foundation for the revered temples we know today."

A Legacy Transcending Time

My father's voice softened as he concluded. "Shanmukha, these sculptures were more than mere stone. They were acts of profound devotion, born from a brother's love and a sage's wisdom. They serve as a timeless reminder that the divine is not confined to temples, but permeates the very fabric of the universe."

I sat in contemplative silence, my young mind swirling with images of the sacred plains, the majestic summit, and the divine sculptures. "What happened to these sites, Father?" I asked, eager for the next chapter of the story.

"That, my dear Shanmukha," he said with a gentle smile, "is a tale for another evening. For now, remember this: the energy of those sculptures continues to resonate throughout the sacred land of Seshachalam, shaping the spiritual landscape of the temples we revere today, a testament to the enduring power of devotion."

Epilogue to Day One: A Night of Contemplation

As my father concluded the tale of Balarama's sculptures and Sukamuni's sanctification, the stars had begun to illuminate the night sky, their celestial light mirroring the divine energy of the story. The gentle rustling of the banyan's leaves seemed to echo the profound truths that had been shared.

"Shanmukha," my father said, his voice soft and steady, "the narrative does not conclude here. There is more to reveal—of how these sacred sites transformed into the temples we hold in reverence today."

"When will you tell me, Father?" I asked, my eagerness palpable.

He smiled, his expression filled with warmth. "Tomorrow, my son. Let the stories settle within you for the night, as we prepare to uncover further truths under the light of a new day."

Reluctantly, I nodded, though my mind was ablaze with questions. As I drifted into sleep that night, visions of Krishna, Balarama, and Sukamuni danced in my dreams, filling me with a sense of awe and anticipation for the stories yet to unfold.

CHAPTER FOUR

THE DIVINE REUNION AT SUKAMUNI ASHRAM

The setting sun painted the sky in hues of gold and crimson, casting elongated shadows that danced across the ancient banyan tree. I waited with bated breath for my father's arrival, the anticipation of continuing the saga filling me with a palpable excitement. As he approached, his serene demeanor and knowing smile calmed my eagerness.

"So, Shanmukha," he began, leaning against the gnarled trunk, "you've been waiting all day to hear more, haven't you?"

"Yes, Father," I admitted, my youthful voice brimming with enthusiasm. "What transpired after Sukamuni sanctified the sculptures? Did Balarama and Krishna reunite?"

My father smiled, his eyes reflecting a distant, cherished memory. "Indeed, my son. Their reunion was as divine as it was profound. Allow me to recount the tale."

Krishna's Quest for Balarama

"Following the Kurukshetra War," my father began, his voice taking on a narrative cadence, "Krishna, having fulfilled his role as Partha Sarathi, felt a profound emptiness in his heart, the absence of his elder brother. Though he had guided Arjuna and upheld dharma, Krishna yearned for Balarama's wisdom and strength."

"Did Krishna know where Balarama was, Father?" I asked, tilting my head in curiosity.

"No, my son," he replied. "Balarama, in his quest for introspection, had embarked on a solitary pilgrimage, leaving no discernible trail. However, Krishna, with his divine intuition, retraced his brother's journey, visiting the sacred sites Balarama had traversed—Prayag, Rameswaram, and finally, the Seshachalam hills."

"Krishna eventually arrived at Sukamuni Ashram," my father continued. "The ashram, bathed in the golden light of the setting sun, seemed to recognize the arrival of divinity itself. Sukamuni, sensing Krishna's presence, emerged to greet him."

"Was Balarama there, Father?" I asked eagerly.

"No, my son," he said. "Balarama had ventured deep into the forest for meditation. Krishna, understanding his brother's need for solitude, chose to await his return."

Yoga Nidra Beneath the Sacred Tree

"While awaiting Balarama's return," my father explained, "Krishna sat beneath a majestic tree near the ashram. Entering a state of Yoga Nidra, he closed his eyes and rested, his form radiating an aura of divine peace. The forest seemed to fall into a reverent silence, as if acknowledging the presence of the Lord."

I imagined the scene, the air thick with a sacred stillness. "What transpired then, Father?" I asked.

"When Balarama returned," he said, "he beheld Krishna resting beneath the tree, his face serene and glowing. Overwhelmed with love and reverence, Balarama chose not to disturb him. Instead, he sat beside his brother, keeping a silent vigil."

Balarama's Contemplations: The Purpose of Krishna's Avatar

My father's voice softened, filled with a deep reverence. "As Balarama watched Krishna in Yoga Nidra, his mind wandered to the very essence of Krishna's avatar. He relived the divine leelas of his brother and the fulfillment of his cosmic mission."

I leaned forward, captivated. "What was the purpose of Krishna's avatar, Father?"

My father smiled, his eyes gleaming with wisdom. "Shanmukha, Krishna descended to Earth for four divine purposes:

1. **To establish dharma**—the harmony of thought, word, and deed. His teachings, particularly the Bhagavad Gita, reminded humanity of the importance of living a life of truth and justice.
2. **To eradicate adharmic forces**—he vanquished the wicked and protected the virtuous, ensuring the balance of good and evil was maintained.
3. **To guide humanity**—through his actions and teachings, Krishna illuminated the path of righteousness, blending compassion, wisdom, and strategic insight.

4. **To restore ecological equilibrium**—the Kurukshetra War, though tragic, served to reduce the population burden and restore balance to the Earth."

The Govardhana Giri Episode

"As Balarama reflected on these purposes," my father continued, "the memory of the Govardhana Giri episode resurfaced—a moment when Krishna demonstrated the importance of respecting nature."

"What occurred at Govardhana Giri, Father?" I asked.

"During their youth in Vrindavan," my father began, "the Yadavs prepared to perform a grand homa to appease Lord Indra, the god of rain. But Krishna, even as a child, questioned their practice. He taught them that it was not Indra, but the earthly resources—the forests, rivers, mountains, and soil—that sustained life and deserved their gratitude."

He continued, his voice steady. "Krishna urged the Yadavs to worship Govardhana Giri, the mountain that provided them with water, grazing lands, and shelter. Angered by this, Indra unleashed a terrible storm. But Krishna, with his divine strength, lifted the mountain on his little finger, sheltering the entire community beneath it for seven days and nights."

The Lesson of Govardhana Giri

"What lesson did Krishna intend to impart, Father?" I asked.

"He sought to demonstrate that nature is sacred," my father replied. "The resources that sustain us—food, water, and shelter—are gifts of the Earth. By honoring and protecting them, we uphold the balance of creation."

He paused, his voice filled with reverence. "Balarama, reflecting on this act, recognized the eternal truth of Krishna's teachings. It was not merely about lifting a mountain; it was about elevating humanity's understanding of what truly matters."

The Sacred Moment of Reunion

"Balarama, contemplating these profound truths, experienced a deep sense of peace," my father continued. "In that moment, he understood that Krishna's mission was not only to guide others, but to transform the universe. The Kurukshetra War, the destruction it wrought, and the peace it restored were all integral parts of the divine plan."

"What did Sukamuni do, Father?" I asked.

"Sukamuni, inspired by their divine bond, decided to immortalize the moment," my father said. "He sculpted an image of Krishna in Yoga Nidra and Balarama sitting beside him in quiet contemplation. This sculpture became a symbol of their eternal connection."

The Reunion of the Divine Brothers

"When Krishna awoke from his Yoga Nidra," my father continued, "he beheld Balarama sitting beside him. The brothers embraced, their bond strengthened. They spent hours together, sharing their thoughts, their experiences, and their hopes for the future."

"What did they discuss, Father?" I asked, my curiosity piqued.

"No one can say for certain," he replied with a smile. "But it is said that their conversation was filled with divine wisdom, shaping the course of dharma for generations to come."

Epilogue to the Second Day: Anticipation of Temples

As the evening deepened into night, the stars began to twinkle in the celestial expanse. My heart was filled with the day's narrative, yet I couldn't help but wonder what the next evening would unveil.

"Father," I asked as we walked back to the house, "will you tell me about the temples tomorrow?"

"Yes, my son," he said, his tone reassuring. "Tomorrow, we will delve into the origins of the sacred temples—the Alaga Perumal Kovil, the Govinda Raja Temple, and the Tirumala Temple."

I nodded, my anticipation already building. The second evening had concluded, but the story was far from its culmination.

CHAPTER FIVE

THE ORIGINS OF ALAGA PERUMAL KOVIL

A hushed anticipation filled the air of the third evening, as if the ancient banyan itself were aware of the unfolding sacred narrative. I sat patiently, my mind replaying the tales of Sukamuni, Balarama, and Krishna. The first stars began to pierce the twilight when my father arrived, his presence radiating a familiar calm.

"Shanmukha," he began, settling into his customary spot beneath the banyan, "tonight, we embark on a pivotal chapter—the origins of the sacred temples of Seshachalam."

I leaned forward, my eagerness palpable. "Are we beginning with the Alaga Perumal Kovil, Father?"

He nodded, a glimmer of reverence in his eyes. "Yes, my son. The temple whose genesis is as enigmatic as it is divine."

The Sacred Moment at Seshachalam's Foothills

"Following the Kurukshetra War," my father began, his voice taking on a narrative cadence, "Krishna, weary from his duties and journey, sought his elder brother, Balarama. Their reunion occurred at Sukamuni Ashram, nestled at the foothills of Seshachalam. Upon Balarama's return from meditation, he found Krishna resting beneath a sacred tree in Yoga Nidra, his form radiating an aura of peace and divinity."

I nodded, recalling the earlier part of the story. "And Balarama sat beside him, correct?"

"Indeed, my son," he said. "Balarama, overwhelmed with love and reverence, sat beside Krishna. His heart was filled with memories of Krishna's leelas—the moments that defined his brother's divine purpose. From lifting Govardhana Giri to guiding Arjuna in the Kurukshetra War, each act played out in his mind like a celestial symphony."

Sukamuni's Divine Revelation

"And Sukamuni witnessed this scene, Father?" I asked, captivated.

"Precisely," he replied, his tone deepening. "Sukamuni, standing a short distance away, beheld this sacred tableau. He saw Krishna in Yoga Nidra, serene and radiant, and Balarama gazing at his brother with boundless love and affection. Sukamuni understood that this was no ordinary sight, but a divine revelation—a moment that encapsulated the essence of their bond and their cosmic purpose."

"What did Sukamuni do, Father?" I asked, leaning closer.

"He resolved," my father continued, "that this moment must be preserved—not just in his memory, but for all of humanity. Guided by divine inspiration, he sculpted vigrahams of Krishna and Balarama, exactly as he had witnessed them."

Sculptures of Divine Love and Manifestation

"Sukamuni's hands," my father said, "were guided by unwavering devotion and divine vision. He sculpted Krishna reclining in Yoga Nidra, his face serene and glowing with cosmic energy. Beside him, he sculpted Balarama, seated with an expression of divine love and admiration, his gaze fixed upon Krishna."

"Were the sculptures crafted from Shaligram stone, Father?" I asked.

"Yes, Shanmukha," he replied with awe. "Sukamuni utilized Shaligram stone, a material not of earthly origin, but believed to carry the very essence of the cosmos. How he obtained it remains a mystery, but the sculptures radiated a divine presence unlike anything previously witnessed."

The Genesis of Alaga Perumal Kovil

"What transpired after Sukamuni sculpted the vigrahams, Father?" I asked eagerly.

"He realized," my father said, "that these vigrahams required a sacred space—a temple where their energy could guide devotees for generations. Sukamuni chose the precise spot where Krishna had rested in Yoga Nidra and Balarama had sat beside him. It was sanctified by their divine presence and by the sacred moment Sukamuni had witnessed."

"And that became the Alaga Perumal Kovil?" I asked.

"Indeed," he replied, nodding. "The temple was named after Krishna as Alaga Perumal, meaning the 'Beautiful Lord.' Sukamuni ensured that the temple captured the essence of that moment—the tranquility of Krishna's repose and the depth of Balarama's devotion."

A Modern Observation and Call to Preservation

"Father," I asked, hesitating slightly, "why don't people recognize this temple as Alaga Perumal Kovil anymore?"

My father's expression grew contemplative. "Shanmukha, this is a matter of regret. The temple, over time, became primarily associated with Goddess Padmavathi, the consort of Lord Venkateswara. While her divine presence has enhanced the temple's sanctity, the name 'Alaga Perumal Kovil' has been largely obscured."

"Even the temple management doesn't acknowledge the name?" I asked, my curiosity tinged with concern.

"No, my son," he said with a sigh. "The Tirumala Tirupati Devasthanam, which manages the temple, officially refers to it only as Sri Padmavathi Ammavari Temple. Nowhere is Alaga Perumal mentioned, despite epigraphical reports clearly inscribing it as Alaga Perumal Kovil. It should be rightfully referred to as Alaga Perumal Sametha Sri Padmavathi Ammavari Temple, honoring its historical significance and preserving the legacy of Krishna, Balarama, and Sukamuni."

"Can this be rectified, Father?" I asked, my voice filled with hope.

"It can, my son," he replied. "If people remember and respect the origins of this temple, if they recognize the importance of preserving its history, then the truth can be restored. The Board of Trustees, appointed by the government under the Act 30 of 1987, has the authority to reinstate the rightful name of this sacred shrine. It is our responsibility, as devotees, to remind them of this duty."

"The Alaga Perumal Kovil," my father continued, "became a place of profound spiritual power. Pilgrims from distant lands came to witness the vigrahams and to feel the divine energy of the brothers' bond. The temple stood as a testament to Sukamuni's devotion and his vision of preserving that sacred moment."

"Does it still carry that energy, Father?" I asked.

"Yes, my son," he said. "Even today, the temple resonates with the energy of that divine moment, preserved by Sukamuni for future generations."

A Legacy for Humanity's Reflection

"The story of Alaga Perumal Kovil," my father concluded, "is a reminder that divinity is not solely found in acts of grandeur, but also in moments of love, devotion, and profound connection. Sukamuni's vision ensured that the bond between Krishna and Balarama would inspire humanity for eternity."

I sat in contemplative silence, the story filling my heart with reverence. "Father," I said, "what about the other temples? The plains and the summit where Balarama sculpted the Partha Sarathi and Viswaroopa?"

"That," he said with a gentle smile, "is a tale for tomorrow. But remember, Shanmukha, that every temple carries a profound lesson for humanity—to honor the divine, to cherish our relationships, and to live in harmony with the universe."

CHAPTER SIX

THE PARTHA SARATHI TO GOVINDA RAJA LEGACY

The soft glow of the moon bathed the ancient banyan in a serene light, and a gentle breeze rustled through its leaves. My father and I sat in quiet anticipation, the air filled with the unspoken reverence of another sacred tale. I could feel the weight of history in my father's demeanor as he prepared to speak.

"Shanmukha," he began, his voice a low, steady murmur, "tonight, we delve into another sacred temple of Seshachalam, a temple that reflects Krishna's role not just as a divine guide, but as the eternal protector of humanity."

"Are we speaking of the Govinda Raja Temple, Father?" I asked.

"Yes, my son," he replied, his gaze drifting into the distance. "But before it became the Govinda Raja Temple, it was known as the Partha Sarathi Temple, established to honor Krishna's role as Arjuna's charioteer during the Kurukshetra War."

The Partha Sarathi Sculpture: A Symbol of Divine Guidance

"Do you recall," my father continued, "how Balarama sculpted Krishna as Partha Sarathi, the divine charioteer?"

"Yes, Father," I said eagerly. "He sculpted it at the plains of Seshachalam."

"Precisely," he replied with a nod. "The sculpture embodied Krishna's role as the ultimate guide, not just to Arjuna, but to all of humanity. It stood as a testament to Krishna's wisdom, his ability to navigate the complexities of life, and his unwavering dedication to dharma."

"Where was the sculpture placed, Father?" I asked.

"It was installed near the northwestern foothills of Sukamuni Ashram," he explained. "A small temple was constructed around it, known as the Partha Sarathi Temple. It became a place of devotion, a reminder of Krishna's teachings in the Bhagavad Gita."

Kulottunga's Remark and the Flight from Chidambaram: A Story of Faith and Peril

"Father," I asked, "how did the idol of Govinda Raja come to Seshachalam?"

My father's expression grew thoughtful. "Ah, Shanmukha, this is a tale of faith and resilience. During the reign of Kulottunga I, an ardent Saivite king, Vaishnavism faced significant challenges. Kulottunga was displeased with the growing prominence of Vaishnavas, and the rivalry between Saivites and Vaishnavites often turned hostile."

"What did Kulottunga do, Father?" I asked hesitantly.

"One day," he began, "Kulottunga visited the renowned Nataraja Temple in Chidambaram. Within the temple complex, he noticed a small shrine dedicated to Vishnu, known as Govinda Raja. Irritated by the perceived arrogance of the Vaishnavas, Kulottunga is said to have remarked that Vishnu's proper place was not on Earth, but in the sea."

My eyes widened. "What happened then?"

"Fearing for the safety of their deity," my father explained, "the Vaishnavas acted swiftly. They walled up the sanctum to protect the idol and secretly fled with the Utsava Murti—the processional idol of Govinda Raja. Traveling through dense forests and avoiding major settlements, they eventually reached the Seshachalam hills, where they sought refuge."

Ramanujacharya's Role in Establishing the Govinda Raja Temple: A Vision of Unity

"It was during this time," my father continued, "that Ramanujacharya emerged as a guiding force. After Kulottunga's reign ended, Ramanuja returned from exile in the Hoyasala kingdom. Upon learning of the idol's journey, he visited Seshachalam and discovered the hidden Utsava Murti of Govinda Raja."

"What did he do, Father?" I asked.

"He recognized the significance of the idol and resolved to establish a proper shrine for it," my father said. "Ramanuja chose to install the idol adjacent to the Partha Sarathi Temple, creating a sacred complex that reflected both Krishna's divine guidance and

Govinda Raja's eternal grace."

The Birth of Tirupati: A Town Founded on Faith

"But, Father," I asked, "how did the settlement around the temple grow into a town?"

"That," my father said with a smile, "was part of Ramanuja's visionary plan. He believed that the establishment of a Brahmin agraharam, or settlement, around the temples would ensure their long-term sustainability. To achieve this, he planned the construction of four Mada Streets around the temple complex and four Raja Streets around the outer periphery. These streets formed the foundation of what we now call Tirupati."

"So, Tirupati was built around the Govinda Raja and Partha Sarathi temples?" I asked.

"Exactly," he replied. "Initially, the town was known as Krishnapuram, then as Govindarajapuram, and eventually as Ramanujapuram in honor of Ramanujacharya. Over time, it came to be known simply as Tirupati."

A Notable Observation: The Forgotten Connection

"Father," I said hesitantly, "is the Govinda Raja Temple still connected to the Partha Sarathi Temple?"

"Unfortunately, my son," he replied, "many of these historical connections have been obscured over time. Today, the Govinda Raja Temple is managed as part of the Tirumala Tirupati Devasthanam (TTD). While it is a place of grandeur and devotion, its original link to the Partha Sarathi Temple and the contributions of the Yadava kings are often overlooked."

"Why is that, Father?" I asked.

"Part of the reason," he explained, "is the lack of widespread awareness about the temple's rich history. The Govinda Raja idol, initially installed alongside Partha Sarathi, became the central focus of the temple, and the Partha Sarathi vigraham is now seen as secondary. It is a poignant reminder, Shanmukha, of the importance of preserving history and honoring those who shaped it."

The Contributions of the Yadava Kings: Unsung Patrons

"But Father," I asked thoughtfully, "how could Ramanuja accomplish so much in such a short period?"

"Ah, my son," he said with a knowing smile, "this was not the work of one man alone. The Yadava kings, including Ghattideva and possibly Yadava Narayana, provided immense support. Their patronage and dedication were instrumental in not only building the Govinda Raja Temple, but also in organizing the rituals at Tirumala and establishing the town of Tirupati."

"So, the Yadava kings played a crucial role in the history of Tirupati?" I asked.

"Indeed," he said. "Without their vision and support, the Govinda Raja Temple, the rituals at Tirumala, and the town of Tirupati itself might never have come into existence."

A Legacy of Faith and Resilience: Echoes of the Past

"The story of the Partha Sarathi and Govinda Raja temples," my father concluded, "is one of faith, resilience, and vision. It reminds us of the divine purpose that Krishna embodied, the strength of Balarama's devotion, and the human efforts of Ramanuja and the Yadava kings to create a legacy that continues to inspire."

I sat in contemplative silence, absorbing the depth of the narrative. "Father," I said finally, "what about the summit of Seshachalam—the Tirumala Temple itself?"

"That," he said with a smile, "is a story for tomorrow. But remember, Shanmukha, that every temple and every act of devotion carries within it the essence of dharma and the enduring spirit of humanity."

32

WHEN GODS WALKED THE SACRED HILLS

CHAPTER SEVEN

THE COSMIC ENERGY OF VENKATESWARA

The fifth evening arrived with an air of divine anticipation, as if the very hills of Seshachalam were whispering tales of devotion and dharma. I sat beneath the ancient banyan, my heart filled with eagerness to hear more.

My father joined me, his presence radiating a familiar serenity. He settled into his usual spot and looked at me with a knowing smile. "Shanmukha," he began, "tonight, we will explore the origins of the most revered temple on the summit of Seshachalam—the temple of Lord Venkateswara."

I straightened, my eyes wide with curiosity. "The Tirumala Temple, Father?"

"Yes," he replied, his tone reverent. "The temple that embodies the cosmic energy of Vishnu, the preserver of the universe. But its story, my son, is as much about humanity as it is about divinity."

The Viswaroopa Sculpture: A Symbol of Universal Energy

"Do you recall," my father began, "how Balarama sculpted the Viswaroopa of Krishna on the summit of Seshachalam?"

"Yes, Father," I said eagerly. "He created it to represent Krishna's cosmic form, didn't he?"

"Exactly," he said. "The sculpture was not merely an artistic creation; it was a representation of universal energy, the divinity that connects all life. Balarama, with his divine intuition, chose the summit of Seshachalam as the site for this sculpture, believing it to be the spiritual axis of the Earth."

"Why did he choose the summit, Father?" I asked.

"Because, Shanmukha," he explained, "the summit symbolized elevation, both physical and spiritual. It was a place where the divine and the mortal could converge, a site of ultimate connection between the heavens and the Earth."

Sukamuni's Sanctification: A Beacon of Spirituality

"What happened to the sculpture after Balarama created it?" I asked.

"It was Sukamuni," my father said, "who sanctified the site. He recognized the cosmic energy of the sculpture and declared the summit as a place of eternal worship. Sukamuni believed that the

Viswaroopa of Krishna would inspire humanity to see the divine in all aspects of life."

"So, the summit became sacred because of Sukamuni's vision?" I asked.

"Yes," he replied. "Sukamuni's wisdom ensured that the summit of Seshachalam would become a beacon of spirituality, a place where seekers could connect with the divine."

The Convergence of Faiths: Conflict and Resolution

"After Sukamuni's time," my father explained, "the sacred summit of Seshachalam underwent many transformations. At different times, it was revered by tribal communities as the abode of a tribal deity, by Shaktheyas as Maa Durga or Bala Tripura Sundari, by Shaivites as Lord Shiva, and by Vaishnavites as Lord Balaji, the preserver of the universe."

"But such diversity must have led to conflicts," I said thoughtfully.

"Indeed, it did," my father replied. "During the reign of the Yadava Rayas, the Shaivites and Vaishnavites clashed fiercely over the temple's identity. Each group claimed the deity as their own, and the conflict escalated into a major crisis."

"What did the Yadava Rayas do, Father?" I asked.

"They realized," he said, "that this conflict threatened not just the sanctity of the temple but also the harmony of their kingdom. To resolve the matter, the Yadava Rayas turned to their Raja Guru, Sriman Ramanuja, a visionary leader and spiritual guide."

The Declaration of Lord Venkateswara: A Divine Revelation

"Ramanuja," my father continued, "arrived at the temple with a profound sense of purpose. He observed the rituals, listened to the grievances of both Shaivites and Vaishnavites, and meditated deeply at the summit. It is said that during his meditation, Lord

Venkateswara himself appeared before him."

"What did the Lord say, Father?" I asked, my heart racing.

"Lord Venkateswara," he said, his voice filled with reverence, "revealed his true identity as Vishnu, the preserver of the universe. He declared that the temple was his abode and that it should be dedicated to guiding humanity towards dharma and spiritual awakening."

"What did Ramanuja do after the revelation?" I asked.

"With the Lord's blessing," my father said, "Ramanuja presented Sudarshana Chakra and Panchajanya, the sacred discus and conch, to Lord Venkateswara. From that moment onward, the deity came to be depicted with four hands—Kati Hasta, Varada Hasta, and two hands holding the Shankha and Chakra."

"Is that why we see Lord Venkateswara with four hands today?" I asked, marveling at the imagery.

"Yes, Shanmukha," he said with a smile. "Ramanuja's act symbolized the divine authority and completeness of Lord Venkateswara. It reaffirmed his role as the cosmic preserver, guiding humanity through all dimensions of existence."

The Resolution of Conflict: Unity in Devotion

"With the Lord's declaration and Ramanuja's wisdom," my father continued, "the conflict between Shaivites and Vaishnavites was resolved. Both groups accepted the temple as the abode of Lord Venkateswara and united in their devotion."

"And the temple became a Vaishnavite shrine from that day?" I asked.

"Yes," he replied. "The temple was established as a center of Vaishnavite worship, but it continued to honor the cosmic energy that had drawn people of all beliefs."

The Yadava Rayas: Patrons of Dharma

"Father," I asked, "how did the Yadava Rayas support the temple after this?"

"The Yadava Rayas," he explained, "played a pivotal role in formalizing the temple's rituals and administration. They provided resources, appointed priests, and ensured that the temple became a center of devotion and dharma. Their contributions laid the foundation for the temple's prominence as one of the most sacred sites in the world."

A Divine Legacy: Enduring Wisdom

"The story of the Tirumala Temple," my father concluded, "is not just about its past. It is a living legacy, a testament to the vision of Sukamuni, the devotion of Balarama, the wisdom of Ramanuja, and the dedication of the Yadava Rayas. It is a reminder that the divine is always present, guiding us through the complexities of life."

I sat in silence, overwhelmed by the depth of the story. "Father," I said finally, "is there more to learn about the temples of Seshachalam?"

"There is always more to learn, Shanmukha," he replied with a gentle smile. "But for tonight, let us rest, knowing that we carry the stories of these sacred temples in our hearts, and that the cosmic energy of Venkateswara continues to bless all who seek his grace."

CHAPTER EIGHT

The Spiritual Significance of Tirupati's Temples

The sixth evening arrived, draped in a soft, golden light as the sun gently descended behind the Seshachalam hills. The tranquility of the moment felt like a sacred invitation to delve deeper into the profound narratives my father had been weaving. I sat beneath the ancient banyan, the lingering scent of jasmine filling the air, eagerly awaiting his arrival.

When he joined me, his presence was as calming as the twilight itself. He settled beside me, the edges of his white shirt glowing softly in the fading light. His face held a gentle smile as he gazed at me.

"Shanmukha," he began, "tonight, we will explore not just individual temples, but the unifying spirit that binds them all. These temples, my son, are more than mere architectural structures—they are living embodiments of grace, strength, and cosmic energy."

The Trinity of Divine Manifestations

"What do you mean, Father?" I asked, leaning closer.

He clasped his hands, his voice taking on a reverent tone. "Each temple in Tirupati carries a unique spiritual essence, Shanmukha. The Alaga Perumal Kovil represents divine grace, the Govinda Raja Temple embodies strength, and the Venkateswara Temple radiates cosmic energy. Together, they form a sacred trinity that guides humanity through life's trials."

"How are they interconnected, Father?" I asked, intrigued.

"They are like the rivers that flow to meet the ocean," he said, his gaze lifting to the heavens. "Each offers a different path, but their ultimate purpose is the same: to lead us to dharma, to inspire unwavering faith, and to remind us of our eternal connection with the divine."

The Grace of Alaga Perumal: A Sanctuary of Divine Love

"Let us begin with the Alaga Perumal Kovil," he said, his tone filled with reverence. "Do you recall how Sukamuni sculpted the vigrahams of Krishna and Balarama in divine unity?"

"Yes, Father," I said eagerly. "He captured Krishna in Yoga Nidra and Balarama gazing at him with love and devotion."

"That vigraham," my father continued, "is a symbol of divine grace—the boundless grace that Krishna extends to all who seek refuge in him. The Alaga Perumal Kovil, now known as the Sri Padmavathi Ammavari Temple, stands as a reminder of Krishna's eternal love and Balarama's selfless devotion."

"But, Father," I interjected, "why is it no longer referred to as the Alaga Perumal Kovil?"

My father sighed, a shadow of thoughtful contemplation crossing his face. "It is a matter of preserving historical accuracy, Shanmukha. Though the temple is now primarily associated with Sri Padmavathi, its origins as the Alaga Perumal Kovil should never be forgotten. It was Sukamuni's visionary insight and the divine bond of the brothers that gave it life."

The Strength of Govinda Raja: A Beacon of Resilience

"What about the Govinda Raja Temple, Father?" I asked.

"Ah, Govinda Raja," he said, his voice filled with admiration. "This temple embodies the strength of devotion and the resilience of unwavering faith. The idol of Govinda Raja, brought from Chidambaram under perilous circumstances, symbolizes the unyielding spirit of the Vaishnavas and the profound wisdom of Ramanujacharya."

"It was Ramanuja who gave it a home next to the Partha Sarathi Temple, wasn't it?" I asked.

"Yes," he replied with a nod. "By placing Govinda Raja beside Partha Sarathi, Ramanuja united two essential aspects of Krishna's divine mission—guidance and strength. The temple became a beacon of hope, teaching devotees to stand firm in the face of adversity."

The Cosmic Energy of Venkateswara: A Nexus of Divinity

"And the Venkateswara Temple, Father?" I asked, my voice filled with awe.

"That," he said with a gentle smile, "is the crown jewel of Seshachalam, the temple where the cosmic energy of Vishnu radiates with unparalleled force. It is a place where the divine and the mortal converge, where humanity finds solace in the eternal presence of the preserver."

"Is it because of the Viswaroopa sculpture that Balarama created?" I asked.

"Partly, yes," he said. "But the temple's profound power lies in its divine purpose. Lord Venkateswara is a manifestation of dharma itself, a guiding light for those who have lost their way, a protector for those who seek refuge, and a constant reminder of the cosmic energy that sustains the universe."

A Symphony of Spiritual Harmony

"So, Father," I said thoughtfully, "each temple represents a different facet of the divine?"

"Exactly, my son," he replied. "The Alaga Perumal Kovil teaches us about grace—the unconditional love of the divine. The Govinda Raja Temple reminds us of strength—the power of resilience and unwavering devotion. And the Venkateswara Temple inspires us to embrace the cosmic energy that connects us to the universe."

"They are like a symphony," I said, marveling at the thought.

"Indeed," he said with a smile. "Each note is distinct, yet together, they create a harmonious melody that uplifts the soul."

A Legacy for Generations: Enduring Spiritual Wisdom

"Father," I asked, "what can we learn from these temples today?"

"We learn, Shanmukha," he said, his voice filled with emotion, "that faith transcends time and place. These temples are a sacred legacy, a gift from those who came before us, reminding us of our divine purpose. They teach us to embrace grace, stand with strength, and live with a profound awareness of our connection to the cosmic energy."

A Sacred Bond: The Enduring Connection

As the night deepened, my father's words lingered in the air like a sacred mantra. "Shanmukha," he said softly, "the temples of Tirupati are not merely places of worship. They are guides, companions, and constant reminders of our eternal bond with the divine."

I sat in contemplative silence, the weight of his words filling my heart with a newfound sense of devotion. "Father," I said finally, "thank you for sharing these stories with me."

He smiled, his eyes glimmering with pride. "It is my duty, my son, to pass on these tales. And it is your duty to carry them forward, so that the enduring legacy of these sacred temples lives on, enriching the lives of generations to come."

THE CULTURAL AND HISTORICAL IMPACT OF TIRUPATI'S TEMPLES

The seventh evening descended upon the Seshachalam hills with a serene elegance, as if the heavens themselves were attuned to the sacred stories being told. The ancient banyan tree, under which my father and I sat, seemed to stand taller, a silent witness to the legacy of faith, art, and service that had been etched into the annals of Tirupati's temples.

My father's face held an expression of both pride and deep contemplation as he began. "Shanmukha," he said, his voice steady and warm, "we have explored the spiritual essence of these temples, but tonight, we shall delve into their profound cultural and historical significance. These temples are not merely sanctuaries for devotion—they are the very foundation upon which art, education, and social service flourished, shaping the cultural identity of an entire region."

Temples as Patrons of Artistic Expression

"Father," I asked, leaning closer, "how did the temples influence the development of art?"

"The temples of Tirupati," he began, "have always been vibrant centers of artistic expression. The intricate carvings adorning their walls, the majestic gopurams reaching towards the heavens, and the lifelike sculptures that grace their sanctums are all masterpieces that narrate divine stories."

His gaze turned wistful as he continued. "The carvings often depict pivotal moments from Krishna's leelas, Balarama's strength, and the cosmic energy of Lord Venkateswara. These depictions are not merely ornamental; they are visual scriptures, imparting the principles of dharma to devotees who may not have access to written texts."

"Did the temples provide support to the artists, Father?" I asked.

"Absolutely," he said with a nod. "The Yadava Rayas and the temple administration nurtured sculptors, painters, and craftsmen, commissioning them to create works of profound devotion. These artists were granted not only patronage but also reverence, as their art was perceived as a form of sacred prayer."

Music and Dance: The Divine Arts of Expression

"And what about music and dance, Father?" I asked.

"The temples were the heart of these divine arts," he replied, his voice filled with admiration. "Bharatanatyam, performed by devadasis within the sanctum, narrated the cosmic dance of Krishna and the sacred stories of Venkateswara. Musicians sang keerthanas and bhajans, their voices rising like celestial offerings to the divine."

"Did these traditions endure across generations?" I asked eagerly.

"Yes, my son," he said. "Saint Annamacharya, for example, composed over 30,000 keerthanas in praise of Lord Venkateswara. His songs continue to resonate within the temple halls, binding generations in shared devotion. The melodies of the veena and the rhythms of the mridangam have been preserved as living traditions, passed down from teacher to student."

Centers of Education and Scholarly Knowledge

"Father," I said thoughtfully, "did these temples also function as centers of learning?"

"Indeed, they did," he replied, his tone filled with pride. "The temples were repositories of Vedic knowledge, philosophy, and literature. Scholars gathered here to study, debate, and share their wisdom with eager students. They imparted not only spiritual knowledge but also astronomy, mathematics, and architecture."

"How did this knowledge shape society, Father?" I asked.

"The wisdom disseminated from these temples," he said, "helped cultivate a culture of understanding and innovation. The very construction of these temples, with their advanced engineering and alignment with celestial bodies, stands as a testament to their mastery of both science and spirituality."

Guardians of Social Welfare and Community Unity

"Father," I asked, "how did the temples serve the wider community?"

"They were pillars of social welfare," he said, his voice filled with respect. "The tradition of annadanam ensured that no devotee left hungry. The temples procured grains and produce from local farmers, bolstering the agrarian economy. During times of famine or calamity, they opened their granaries and provided shelter to those in need."

"Did the temples play a role in fostering unity among the people?" I asked.

"Yes, my son," he replied. "The rituals, festivals, and daily practices brought people together, transcending social and economic divisions. The temples became spaces where humanity gathered in shared devotion, bound by a common spiritual purpose."

A Legacy of Resilience and Enduring Faith

"Father," I said, "these temples have stood for centuries despite numerous challenges. How have they endured?"

"Through unwavering faith and remarkable resilience," he replied. "These temples have weathered invasions, natural disasters, and political upheavals. But the steadfast devotion of the people and the unwavering dedication of the temple administrators ensured their survival. They stand today as symbols of our collective spirit and our enduring faith."

An Everlasting Influence on Regional Culture

"Father," I asked, "what is the lasting impact of these temples on our culture?"

"The temples of Tirupati," he said, "have profoundly shaped not only the culture of this region but also the very identity of its people. Through their art, music, rituals, and acts of service, they remind us of our rich divine heritage and inspire us to live with purpose and integrity."

"They are more than mere monuments," I said, reflecting on his profound words.

"Yes, Shanmukha," he said, his voice filled with emotion. "They are living legacies—vessels of grace, strength, and cosmic energy. They teach us to honor our past, embrace our present, and build a future rooted in the principles of dharma."

A Sacred Responsibility to Uphold Tradition

As the evening deepened, my father's words lingered in the air like a sacred chant. "Shanmukha," he said softly, "these temples are not just gifts from our ancestors. They are sacred responsibilities that we must uphold. By preserving their stories, their traditions, and their timeless lessons, we ensure that their guiding light continues to illuminate humanity."

I nodded, my heart swelling with pride and reverence. "Father," I said, "I will carry these stories forward."

He smiled, placing a comforting hand on my shoulder. "That is all I ask, my son. The enduring legacy of these temples lives on through you and through all those who will come after you."

As the night enveloped us, the stories of art, education, and service resonated deeply within me. I understood that the temples of Tirupati were not merely architectural structures; they were vibrant sanctuaries of culture, devotion, and humanity, eternally connected to the divine.

CHAPTER TEN

The Rituals and Festivals of Tirupati's Temples

The eighth evening arrived, the air fragrant with the delicate perfume of jasmine and alive with the distant, resonant peal of temple bells. The ancient banyan, beneath which we sat, seemed to possess a vibrant energy, its roots anchoring centuries of history while its branches reached skyward—much like the rituals and festivals of Tirupati's temples, profoundly rooted in tradition yet aspiring to unite humanity with the divine.

My father settled beside me, the tranquil glow of twilight illuminating his face. His voice, carrying a gentle reverence, began to weave its tale. "Shanmukha," he said, "the temples of Tirupati are not merely physical spaces of worship. They are brought to life by their vibrant rituals and festivals, each a sacred dialogue with the divine, a bridge connecting millions of devotees across the vast expanse of time and space."

The Daily Rituals: A Rhythmic Pulse of Devotion

"Father," I asked, "what kind of rituals are performed in these temples each day?"

"The daily rituals," he began, "are like the rhythmic heartbeat of these sacred spaces, each act pulsating with unwavering devotion. The day commences before the first light of dawn with the Suprabhatam—a gentle hymn that awakens the Lord from his divine slumber. This is followed by the Abhishekam, a ceremonial bath where the deity is lovingly bathed in sacred waters and a fragrant blend of milk, curd, honey, and sandalwood paste."

"What follows the Abhishekam, Father?" I inquired, my curiosity growing.

"After the Abhishekam, we have the Thomala Seva, where the Lord is adorned with garlands of fresh flowers. Then, the Archana is performed, during which the 1008 names of Lord Venkateswara are chanted, accompanied by the offering of flowers. Following this, the Naivedyam is offered, where the Lord is presented with various food items prepared with utmost purity. Then the Sahasra Deepalankarana Seva is performed in the evening, where thousands of lamps are lit, creating a divine spectacle."

"Is it akin to the Lord's daily routine?" I asked, my mind picturing the scene.

"Precisely," he replied, a warm smile gracing his lips. "These rituals mirror the life of a devotee—waking, bathing, nourishing, and resting. They serve as a constant reminder that the divine is present in every facet of our lives, not separate from us, but intimately intertwined with our daily existence."

The Potent Power of Mantras: Invoking the Divine

"Father," I asked, "how significant are mantras in these rituals?"

"Mantras," he said, his voice imbued with reverence, "are the very essence of the rituals. They are ancient, sacred chants that invoke the divine presence, filling the temple with potent, sacred vibrations. Each mantra carries a unique spiritual energy that connects the devotee to the boundless cosmic consciousness."

"Could you share an example, Father?" I asked.

"The mantra 'Om Namo Venkatesaya'," he said, "is seemingly simple, yet profoundly powerful. It is a heartfelt call to Lord Venkateswara, a prayer that dissolves the ego and fills the heart with immeasurable peace. When chanted with sincere devotion, it has the transformative power to purify the mind and uplift the soul. Also the Vishnu Sahasranamamchanting which happens daily, is a powerful tool for devotees."

Brahmotsavam: The Grand Spectacle of Divine Glory

"Father," I asked, "what is the most important festival celebrated in these temples?"

"The Brahmotsavam," he replied, his eyes lighting up with youthful excitement. "It is the grandest of all festivals, celebrated with unparalleled devotion and magnificent grandeur. For nine glorious days, the temple is transformed into a cosmic stage, drawing millions of devotees from every corner of the world."

"Why is it called Brahmotsavam, Father?" I asked.

"It is believed," he explained, "that Lord Brahma himself initiated this sacred festival to honor Lord Venkateswara. The highlight of the Brahmotsavam is the divine procession of the deity on elaborately adorned vahanas, or divine vehicles, each one representing a unique and powerful aspect of divinity. The Ankurarpanam which is the ritual sowing of nine kinds of seeds is performed before the Brahmotsavam starts, symbolizing the beginning of the festival."

"Which vahana is the most special, Father?" I asked.

"The Garuda Vahana," he said, a note of awe resonating in his voice. "On this auspicious day, the Lord is carried in majestic procession on Garuda, his celestial vehicle. The sight is truly divine, a breathtaking representation of strength, unwavering courage, and boundless devotion. Devotees gather in immense numbers, their hearts overflowing with indescribable joy, eager to catch a glimpse of the Lord."

Rathotsavam: The Chariot Festival of Devotion

"Father," I continued, "is there also a chariot festival?"

"Yes," he said, nodding in affirmation. "The Rathotsavam, or Chariot Festival, is another magnificent highlight of the Brahmotsavam celebrations. The deity is placed upon a grand, ornately decorated chariot, adorned with vibrant flowers and dazzling lights, and is pulled through the sacred streets of Tirumala by thousands of devoted pilgrims."

"What does it symbolize, Father?" I asked.

"The chariot," he explained, "represents the human body, while the deity seated within symbolizes the indwelling soul. By pulling the chariot with fervent devotion, devotees demonstrate their unwavering dedication to the divine, seeking liberation from the attachments of the material world and the cycle of rebirth."

The Unifying Spirit of Devotion: A Shared Purpose

"Father," I said thoughtfully, "how do these festivals foster unity among people?"

"These festivals," he said, "are not merely celebrations; they are a powerful testament to the strength of shared faith and unwavering unity. People from all walks of life, regardless of their background or social standing, come together to serve the Lord with selfless devotion, whether by preparing the sacred prasadam, adorning the temple with beautiful decorations, or participating in the vibrant processions. They serve as a poignant reminder that in the divine presence, we are all equal, united by the same eternal spirit that binds us all together."

Timeless Rituals, Eternal Lessons: Enduring Wisdom

"Do these rituals and festivals change over time?" I asked.

"The essence of the rituals," he said, "remains timeless and unchanging. While certain practices may evolve to adapt to the needs of the times, their core purpose remains steadfast: to connect us with the divine, to preserve the profound wisdom of our ancestors, and to inspire us to live our lives with unwavering faith and deep devotion."

A Celebration of Life: Gratitude and Wonder

As the night deepened, my father's words seemed to echo the timeless chants of the temples, their wisdom resonating in the stillness. "Shanmukha," he said softly, his voice filled with gentle warmth, "these rituals and festivals are far more than mere traditions. They are vibrant celebrations of life itself, reminding us to live each day with gratitude, humility, and a profound sense of wonder for the divine mysteries that surround us."

I nodded, feeling the profound weight of his words settle within my heart. "Father," I said, my voice filled with heartfelt gratitude, "thank you for sharing these beautiful stories with me. I feel as though I am seeing the temples in a completely new and illuminating light."

He smiled, his eyes glimmering with pride and affection. "It is my greatest joy, my son, to pass on these sacred tales. And it is now your sacred duty to cherish and preserve them, so that these timeless traditions continue to inspire and uplift generations yet to come, guiding them on their own spiritual journeys."

CHAPTER ELEVEN

The Role of Temples in Contemporary Society

The ninth evening arrived, draped in a profound stillness, as if the very fabric of the universe paused to witness the culmination of a timeless narrative. My father and I sat beneath the familiar banyan tree, the soft moonlight casting ethereal shadows upon the earth. Over the preceding evenings, this ancient tree had borne witness to the unfolding of tales that intricately wove together history, divinity, and the enduring spirit of humanity. Tonight, I sensed that the story was drawing near its final, resonant crescendo.

"Shanmukha," my father began, his voice steady yet imbued with a contemplative depth, "we have journeyed together through the origins, sanctity, and profound spiritual essence of the Tirupati temples. But tonight, I wish to share with you how these sacred spaces continue to shape our world in the present day. They are not merely relics of a bygone era; they are vibrant pillars of contemporary society, guiding us toward a more enlightened and compassionate future."

Temples as Dynamic, Living Institutions

"Father," I asked, "how do these ancient temples remain relevant in a world that has undergone such profound transformations?"

"These temples, Shanmukha," he said, his voice imbued with a gentle reverence, "are not mere edifices of stone and mortar. They are dynamic, living institutions. Through their daily rituals, vibrant festivals, and unwavering commitment to serving the community, they preserve their timeless wisdom while simultaneously addressing the evolving needs of the present."

"But can ancient traditions truly guide us in today's complex world, Father?" I asked, my curiosity piqued.

"Indeed, my son," he replied with unwavering conviction. "Traditions are akin to the deep, strong, and nourishing roots of a banyan tree. They provide the essential foundation that allows the branches to grow, adapt, and spread, just as these temples continue to evolve while remaining firmly anchored in their sacred purpose."

Centers of Unwavering Social Service and Compassion

"Father," I asked, "how do the temples actively serve society?"

"The temples of Tirupati," he explained, "are beacons of selfless service and boundless compassion. Through the renowned annadanam program, they provide sustenance to millions of devotees each day, ensuring that no one leaves the sacred precincts hungry. They also operate hospitals and educational institutions, extending vital care and knowledge to the most vulnerable members of society."

"Do they also respond during times of crisis, Father?" I inquired.

"Yes," he replied with a quiet pride. "During periods of famine, floods, and pandemics, the temples have opened their doors wide, offering food, shelter, and medical aid to those in dire need. Their resources are directed not only towards devotees but to anyone facing hardship, embodying the true essence of dharma."

Guardians of Cultural Heritage and Artistic Expression

"Father," I said thoughtfully, "we have discussed the role of temples in fostering art, music, and dance. Do they still actively promote these cultural expressions?"

"Indeed, my son," he said with a warm smile. "The Tirupati temples remain steadfast patrons of the arts, hosting concerts, festivals, and workshops that preserve and celebrate traditional music, dance, and literature. They provide essential support to artisans and performers, ensuring that our rich cultural heritage is not merely remembered but actively celebrated."

"And what about the preservation of education and knowledge?" I asked.

"The temples continue to serve as vibrant centers of learning," he said. "They provide funding for scholarships to deserving students, support research into ancient texts, and promote the study of Vedas, Agamas, and temple architecture. These dedicated efforts ensure that the profound wisdom of our ancestors is passed on to future generations."

A Unifying Force in a Divided World

"Father," I asked, "do the temples serve as a unifying force, bringing people together?"

"They do, Shanmukha," he said, his eyes glowing with a quiet pride. "In a world often fractured by divisions of caste, creed, and nationality, these temples serve as a powerful unifying force. Here, before the divine, everyone is equal, their hearts united in shared devotion. The awe-inspiring sight of millions of people, from all walks of life, coming together in prayer is a testament to the enduring power of faith."

Timeless Lessons for Modern Times: Adapting with Wisdom

"Father," I asked, "what timeless lessons can we learn from these temples in our modern age?"

"They teach us," he said, "to adapt and evolve without compromising our core values, to serve others selflessly, and to preserve that which is sacred. The temples remind us that faith is not a static entity; it grows, evolves, and discovers new ways to inspire and uplift humanity."

"Will they endure, Father?" I asked, my voice filled with a hopeful anticipation.

"They will, my son," he replied with a quiet confidence. "As long as there are individuals who cherish their legacy, and as long as hearts beat with unwavering devotion, these temples will continue to endure. It is our sacred responsibility to be their guardians, to ensure that their guiding light continues to shine brightly."

The Final, Enduring Lesson: A Legacy of Light

As the evening deepened into the stillness of night, my father's voice softened, imbued with a gentle warmth. "Shanmukha," he said, "this is the final story I will share with you beneath this ancient banyan tree. But remember, this is not the end. The enduring legacy of these temples, and the profound lessons they carry, will remain with you always."

I looked at him, my heart filled with a bittersweet gratitude. "Thank you, Nanna," I said, my voice trembling with emotion. "For every story, every word, and every precious moment. You have given me a gift that I will cherish for a lifetime."

He smiled, his eyes filled with a deep affection and pride. "Remember, my son," he said, "these stories are not just ours. They belong to everyone. It is your sacred duty to share them, to preserve them, and to live your life guided by their timeless wisdom."

With those final words, the storytelling that had become the rhythmic heartbeat of our evenings came to a gentle close. Yet, the radiant light of those stories continued to illuminate my path, guiding me through life with unwavering faith, a clear sense of purpose, and an enduring devotion to the sacred legacy of Tirupati.

Epilogue: A Legacy Carried Forward

The ancient banyan, once a steadfast sentinel of our shared evenings, has long since yielded to the passage of time. The Seshachalam hills, bathed in the soft glow of a different sky, stand as silent witnesses to the decades that have unfolded since my father first entrusted me with these sacred narratives. Yet, his voice, his profound wisdom, and his unwavering love resonate within me with an undiminished clarity. For it is said that temples are not merely structures of stone and mortar; they are living repositories of history, culture, and the enduring flame of devotion. And so, too, are the stories we inherit and pass along.

As I sit to commit this tale to paper, I am struck by the enduring power of heritage, its ability to transcend the boundaries of time and space. The temples of Tirupati, more than mere places of worship, stand as powerful symbols of resilience, unity, and divine grace. They are a testament to the gods who once graced these sacred hills with their presence, the sages who sanctified them with their profound wisdom, and the kings who protected them with their unwavering devotion.

My father, with his serene countenance, his clean-shaven face radiating kindness, and his eyes reflecting a gentle understanding, would have smiled to see these stories shared with the world. He always believed in the transformative power of storytelling—not merely as a means to preserve the echoes of the past, but as a guiding light to illuminate the path toward a more enlightened future.

And so, this book, this humble offering, is not solely mine. It belongs to every pilgrim who has ascended the sacred steps to Tirumala, their hearts filled with devotion. It belongs to every devotee who has lifted their voice in praise of Lord Venkateswara, their souls resonating with the divine. And it belongs to every child who has sat beneath the sheltering embrace of a tree, their eyes wide with wonder, as their parent wove tales of unwavering faith and indomitable courage.

This is my tribute, a heartfelt offering to the gods who once walked these hallowed hills, leaving their divine footprints upon the earth. It is a tribute to the people who, with their unwavering devotion and tireless dedication, built a legacy that has endured through the ages. And it is, above all, a tribute to the father who instilled in me a deep and abiding belief in the enduring magic of stories.

May these tales, imbued with the sacred essence of Tirupati, inspire you to carry forward this legacy, to preserve the sacred traditions that bind us to our past, and to honor the divine in all its myriad forms. May they ignite within you a spark of understanding, compassion, and unwavering faith, illuminating your own journey with the radiant light of timeless wisdom.

About The Author

Y.S.Yadav, an eminent jurist, author, and social reformer, stands as a stalwart champion of legal enlightenment, equitable justice, and the safeguarding of cultural heritage. Practicing as an advocate in the Andhra Pradesh High Court, he holds esteemed leadership roles as National President of Service Civil International (SCI-India), an organization with consultative status at the UNO & UNESCO, National Secretary of Central Human Rights Organisation, National Executive Member of All India Yadav Mahasabha, and State Secretary of the Indian Association of Lawyers (IAL), Andhra Pradesh.

A prolific wordsmith, his literary oeuvre traverses jurisprudence, historiography, and societal transformation, marrying legal acumen with narrative artistry. Among his notable works are 'The Constitution Speaks: Stories of India's Top 25 Landmark Judgments', 'Golla Mandapam', 'Gopika Geetham', and 'THE ASH-BORN WARRIORS: The Naga Sadhus and the Secrets of the Maha Kumbh'.His recent publication 'The YS Tales: Whispers *of Wisdom'* is a journey of exploration into the depths of human experience and the enduring power of wisdom, Forthcoming volumes '*My Fate - A Journey Beyond Boundaries and Beliefs*' and '*The Gambit of Gandhara*' promise to be thought-provoking additions to his literary repertoire.

Beyond his legal and literary pursuits, Y.S.Yadav is a passionate advocate for the rights of marginalized communities, particularly the OBCs. He champions policy reforms, cultural heritage preservation, and social justice initiatives, striving to create a more equitable and inclusive society.

A firm believer in the mantra "Rise for Rights and Stand for Justice," his mission is to educate, empower, and inspire readers to engage with the law, history, and social issues that shape our world.

Glossary Of Terms

Abhishekam : A Hindu ritual of bathing a deity's idol with sacred substances such as milk, honey, and water as an act of devotion.

Agamas : Ancient scriptures that provide guidelines for temple construction, rituals, and worship practices.

Annadanam : The practice of offering free food to devotees, symbolizing compassion and community service.

Banyan Tree : A large and sacred tree in Hindu culture, often associated with wisdom, spiritual shelter, and eternal growth.

Bhagavad Gita : A sacred Hindu scripture consisting of teachings by Lord Krishna to Arjuna on duty, righteousness, and spirituality.

Bharatanatyam : A classical Indian dance form known for its grace, storytelling, and spiritual significance.

Brahmotsavam : A grand annual festival celebrated in Tirupati and other temples, marked by processions, rituals, and vibrant celebrations.

Chakra (Sudarshana Chakra): The divine discus held by Lord Vishnu, symbolizing the cycle of creation, preservation, and destruction.

Dharma : A core concept in Indian philosophy signifying righteousness, duty, and the moral order of the universe.

Devadasi : A traditional temple dancer in ancient India who dedicated her art to the service of deities.

Divine Leelas : The playful, miraculous, and divine acts performed by deities like Krishna.

Garuda Vahana : The celestial vehicle of Lord Vishnu, represented by Garuda, the divine bird known for strength and devotion.

Gopuram : The towering gateway structure of a South Indian temple, adorned with intricate carvings and sculptures.

Hala : A plough carried by Lord Balarama, symbolizing agricultural prosperity and divine protection.

Kati Hasta : A hand posture of Lord Venkateswara, symbolizing strength and assurance

Kurukshetra War : The epic battle from the Mahabharata, representing the conflict between dharma and adharma.

Mantra : A sacred word or phrase chanted to invoke divine energy and focus the mind.

Moksham : The ultimate liberation or salvation from the cycle of birth and rebirth.

Partha Sarathi : A title of Lord Krishna, meaning the charioteer of Arjuna during the Kurukshetra War.

Panchajanya : The divine conch of Lord Vishnu, symbolizing the sound of creation and victory over evil.

Prasadam : Sanctified food offered to deities and distributed to devotees as a blessing.

Ramanuja: A revered saint and philosopher who contributed to the Vaishnavite tradition and the spiritual development of temples like Tirupati.

Rathotsavam : The chariot festival where the deity is taken on a grand procession, symbolizing divine grace and human dedication.

Shaligram Stone : A sacred stone believed to represent Lord Vishnu, often used in worship and idol construction.

Shaivites and Vaishnavites : Two major sects in Hinduism, devoted respectively to Lord Shiva and Lord Vishnu.

Suprabhatam : A morning hymn sung to awaken the deity, symbolizing a new day of devotion.

Tiruppavai : A set of devotional hymns composed by Andal, celebrating devotion to Lord Vishnu.

Vahanas : Vehicles or mounts of deities, symbolizing their divine attributes and powers.

Vaishnavism : A tradition within Hinduism devoted to the worship of Lord Vishnu and his incarnations.

Vigraham : An idol or image of a deity used for worship in temples.

Viswaroopa : The cosmic form of Lord Krishna, representing the infinite energy of the universe.

Glossary of Words and Their Meanings

Abode : A place where someone resides, often used in a spiritual context to describe a divine dwelling.

Adorned : Decorated or embellished, often with beautiful or elaborate details.

Amidst : In the middle of or surrounded by.

Annals : Historical records or chronicles of events.

Ardent : Passionate or enthusiastic, showing intense devotion or eagerness.

Auspicious : Conducive to success or favorable, often associated with good fortune.

Beacon : A guiding light or inspiration, often used metaphorically.

Celestial : Pertaining to the heavens or the divine, beyond the earthly realm.

Chronicled : Recorded in a detailed or historical manner.

Compassion : A feeling of deep sympathy and concern for the suffering of others, accompanied by a desire to help.

Converge : To come together from different directions to meet at a point.

Cosmic : Relating to the universe or its vastness, often associated with the divine.

Depicted : Represented visually or described in detail.

Devotion : Deep love, loyalty, or commitment, often in a spiritual or religious sense.

Divinity : The state of being divine, godlike, or sacred.

Eternal : Lasting forever, without beginning or end.

Exquisite : Extremely beautiful and finely detailed.

Faith : A strong belief or trust in something, especially in a spiritual or religious context.

Fervor : Intense passion or enthusiasm.

Guidance: Advice or direction provided to help navigate challenges or decisions.

Hallowed : Greatly revered or respected; regarded as sacred.

Heritage : The traditions, values, and history passed down from previous generations.

Illuminates : Sheds light on or makes something clear and understandable.

Imbued : Permeated or filled with a particular quality or feeling.

Inscribe : To write or engrave words, often on a surface such as stone or metal.

Inspire : To fill someone with the urge or ability to do something creative or meaningful.

Legacy : Something handed down from the past, such as traditions, values, or achievements.

Majestic : Having beauty, dignity, or grandeur.

Narrative : A story or account of events, either factual or fictional.

Ordinary : Commonplace or not exceptional; regular.

Panoramic : A wide, all encompassing view, often used to describe landscapes or perspectives.

Pilgrimage : A journey to a sacred place for religious or spiritual purposes.

Profound : Deep and meaningful, often in a spiritual or intellectual way.

Radiate : To emit energy or light, often metaphorically used to describe a strong presence or emotion.

Reverence : Deep respect and admiration, often for something sacred or divine.

Sanctified : Made holy or set apart for sacred use.

Serene : Calm, peaceful, and untroubled.

Significance : The importance or meaning of something, often with deeper implications.

Solace : Comfort or consolation in a time of distress or sadness.

Spiritual : Relating to the soul, spirit, or deeper aspects of existence beyond the physical.

Steadfast : Resolutely firm and unwavering.

Symbolize : To represent something through symbols, images, or actions.

Tranquility : A state of peace and calmness.